The Grey Striped Shirt

How Grandma and Grandpa Survived the Holocaust

by Jacqueline Jules

Illustrations by Michael Cressy

Alef Design Group

ISBN # 0-831283–06–2

Published by Alef Design Group

Library of Congress Cataloging-in-Publication Data

Jules, Jacqueline, 1956–
      The grey striped shirt : how Grandma and Grandpa survived the Holocaust / by Jacqueline Jules.
      Summary: When Frannie finds a grey striped shirt in the closet, she asks questions which lead her grandparents to tell her about their experiences of the Holocaust.
      ISBN 1-881283-06-2 : $13.95
      1. Holocaust, Jewish (1939-1945)—Juvenile fiction. [1. Holocaust, Jewish (1939-1945)—Fiction. 2. Grandparents—Fiction.]   I. Title.
      PZ7.J92947Gr   1993
      [Fic]—dc20
                                                                                              93-46902
                                                                                              CIP
                                                                                              AC

Bt 13.95/12.00 5/95

Alef Design Group
4423 Fruitland Avenue
Los Angeles, California 90058
(213) 582-1200

To those who rebuilt their lives and
created new families after suffering
unbearable loss and hardship.
Such courage is an inspiration to us all.

rannie!" Grandma Trudie called that Saturday morning from the top of the stairs. "Did you find my purple hat with the feather?"

"No," I called back, "but I found a red hat with a feather and a blue one with a veil."

Grandma Trudie's large cedar closet had at least fifteen boxes holding fifteen different kinds and colors of ladies' hats.

"Look underneath the dresses," Grandma Trudie shouted. "It's in a round box."

It was hard to see at first. I had to push away a heavy overcoat and a tan dress with brown fur around the hem. But in the back corner, underneath a long and dusty velvet dress, was a round box. I crawled on my hands and knees to bring it to the front of the closet.

Then I sneezed. The dust on top of the box was just too much for my nose. I sneezed again and again as I lifted the lid. With all my sneezing I didn't realize that the thing I was lifting out of the box was not one of my grandmother's hats. It was a grey striped shirt.

"Frannie!" Grandpa Herman called this time. "You can come now. Trudie found her purple hat. It was in the bedroom closet." I dropped the grey striped shirt and ran upstairs. I wasn't sure why, but I didn't want my grandfather to know what I had been looking at.

When we finally walked out the door that Shabbat morning, Grandma Trudie had a question for me.

"Did I ever tell you why I am so fond of hats?"

"Because her father was in the hat business," Grandpa Herman answered.

"Shush." Grandma Trudie touched my grandfather's arm.

"This is my story. Frannie always listens to your stories when she comes to visit. It's time for her to hear mine."

"All right, I'll be quiet." Grandpa Herman folded his hands behind his back and stepped onto the sidewalk.

i love hats," Grandma Trudie began, "because my father owned a ladies' hat shop in Germany where I grew up. I remember what a special treat it was to be allowed to spend the day in my father's shop. While he was busy with his customers my two sisters and I would play in the storeroom in front of a long mirror propped against the wall. We would pretend that we were royal ladies choosing hats for important occasions. The game could go on for hours as we curtsied to each other and the mirror many times.

"My father knew we played with his hats in the storeroom but he didn't mind. He said it was good practice for us. He wanted his three little girls to grow up to be fashionable ladies who always wore hats to match their dresses."

"And that's why you like hats?" I asked.

"Yes," Grandma Trudie said, "because it reminds me of my father's shop and my sisters and the happy times I had growing up as a child. We lived in a beautiful town called Heidelberg. It lies on a river and is surrounded by gently sloping

hills filled with trees. But the prettiest sight there, in my mind, sits high above the town. It is the famous Heidelberg Castle."

When Grandma Trudie said the word "castle," a wonderful picture came to my mind of a princess looking out of a tall tower at a beautiful garden and a drawbridge with a moat. Castles were things you heard about in fairy tales!

"Why would you ever leave a place that had its very own castle?" I asked.

My question startled Grandma Trudie. Her mouth fell open, and she stopped talking for a minute. When she finally did answer me, she spoke slowly, as if she were thinking very carefully about every word she said.

"My family and I left Germany because a man named Adolf Hitler gained control of the government. He passed laws which took German citizenship and jobs away from Jewish people. My father thought we would be better off if we went to Holland, where we had relatives. Then World War II started, and German troops took over almost all of Europe. It turned out that we were no safer in Holland than we had been in Germany."

I didn't know what to say after Grandma Trudie told me about leaving Germany because of Adolf Hitler. The tone of her voice was so serious and sad, it scared me. I was glad when we turned the corner onto the tree-lined street that led to my grandparents' synagogue.

"Look above you!" Grandpa Herman said. "See those branches!"

Grandma Trudie and I looked up to see tall trees on either side of the street bending over in a beautiful green arch. "It's like a _huppah_, a marriage canopy," Grandma Trudie said.

"Yes, it is," Grandpa Herman said as he took both my hands in his. "And it reminds me of the big goal I have in my life now. Can you guess what it is, Frannie?"

I shook my head and giggled. Grandpa Herman was suddenly in

one of his silly moods. I could tell by the way his face wrinkled up at his eyes.

"My dream is to live long enough to dance at my granddaughter's wedding."

"Grandpa!" I laughed as he whirled me around in a little dance on the sidewalk. "How can you talk about my wedding? I'm only nine years old!"

"Never laugh at the future, Frannie," he said. "Hope is a weapon against bad times."

With my grandmother walking behind us, shaking her head and smiling, Grandpa Herman and I danced down the block to the synagogue steps.

My grandparents had many friends at their synagogue. After services, at the Kiddush of wine and cookies, I was kissed by at least eight white-haired ladies who told me I'd grown five inches since the last time I came to visit. Then a man told me in a very loud voice that I was a bee-yoo-tiful little girl. That embarrassed me. I whispered to my grandmother that I had to go to the ladies room.

In the hallway I stopped to look at a long row of pictures I didn't remember seeing before. Both my grandparents were there. Their names were written in shining gold plaques I touched with my finger.

Herman Zelkowicz,
synagogue president,
1968-1970.

Trudie Zelkowicz,
Sisterhood president,
1972-1974.

In the picture Grandma Trudie had dark brown hair which she wore in a puffed-up hairstyle. Grandpa Herman looked very

handsome without wrinkles on his face.

I liked seeing what my grandparents looked like a long time ago, before I was born. No one ever told me they had been presidents at their synagogue. It was nice finding out.

hen we got home from services we had a light lunch of gefilte fish and <u>h</u>allah. Then my grandparents went upstairs to take a nap the way they always did on Shabbat afternoons. I was supposed to be reading quietly in my room or taking a nap myself. But I had something else on my mind. Very slowly, so it wouldn't creak the least little bit, I opened the door to the basement and tiptoed down the stairs to the cedar closet.

I sat on the floor for a long time, looking at the grey striped shirt. It was made of a scratchy kind of material and it had many stains. There was also a place on the left sleeve where a ragged hole had been sewn up. It was certainly not like any of the other clothes Grandma Trudie kept in the cedar closet. Those clothes were worn on special dressy occasions. This looked like it had been used for very hard and dirty work.

After a while I decided to try it on, even though I knew it would be too big. There was a mirror hanging on the door of the cedar closet. I could see exactly what I looked like.

I looked like a prisoner in a jail.

Why did my grandparents have a
prison uniform in their cedar closet?
I knew they had been in something
called a concentration camp during
a war, but I didn't think it was like a
real prison with uniforms and
everything. I couldn't imagine either
one of my grandparents as a
prisoner in a jail.

Part of me wanted to run upstairs
with the grey striped shirt and ask
my grandparents all about it.
Another part of me wasn't sure. My
parents had told me once that what
Grandma Trudie and Grandpa
Herman had suffered during the war
was the kind of thing of which
nightmares were made. I didn't
want nightmares. So I put the

uniform back inside the box and
under the long velvet dress in the
far corner of the closet.

t sundown, when it was time for *Havdalah*, the service which ends the Sabbath, Grandpa Herman said something I had been waiting to hear for a long time.

"Frannie, you are old enough now. Why don't you hold the candle?"

I took the pretty braided candle and held it steady while Grandpa Herman lit all six wicks on top. The flame was high and very bright in

the dark room. A little kid might drop it and burn herself. But I held the candle very straight while Grandpa Herman recited the blessings.

After we had all smelled the spicebox and taken a sip of wine, we sang *Eliyahu ha-Navi*, the song about the prophet Elijah coming with the Messiah and bringing on a perfect world. The melody was sweet, like the smell of the spices. I could've gone on singing a lot longer than we did.

Then my grandfather lit another match in the dining room. This time it was for a *yahrzeit* candle in memory of his sister who had died on that day many years ago. A small circle of light rose from the little candle to shine on the ceiling as Grandpa Herman said the Kaddish, the prayer for the dead. When he was through he took a handkerchief out of his pocket and blew his nose loudly. I wasn't surprised to see him cry. Even though I only visited once every month or so, I had seen this many times. Grandpa Herman says Kaddish for thirty-four relatives every year. Grandma Trudie says Kaddish for forty-nine. They always cry when they light the candles.

ow did your sister die?" I asked Grandpa Herman a few minutes later. We were sitting at the kitchen table, drinking our favorite bedtime treat—chocolate Ovaltine.

"She died because we had no food," Grandpa Herman answered quietly.

"Why didn't you have food?" I asked. "Were you poor?"

Grandpa Herman put down his cup of Ovaltine. His brown eyes

looked directly into mine. He spoke slowly, in a deep voice.

"All Jews were poor then. It was during World War II. Germany invaded my country of Poland. Nazis—soldiers loyal to Hitler—took power. They forced Jews out of their homes and into ghettos. These were small rundown sections of certain cities closed in on all sides by a fence or a wall. The ghettos were unbearably crowded. My family of six had to share our apartment with other families. Sometimes as many as ten people slept on the floor of one room.

"We were given a little bread and a few potatoes about once a week. We rarely saw meat or green

vegetables. My youngest sister, Esther, was only two years old when the war started. She didn't remember ever tasting chocolate or ice cream. She didn't know what it was like to eat an apple. She only knew hunger. Hunger so bad it caused illness and death."

"What about grocery stores?" I asked. "Didn't you have any?"

Grandpa Herman shook his head.

"There were no grocery stores inside the ghetto. But it was possible to sneak out and buy food. They called this smuggling. It was very dangerous. There were soldiers guarding the ghetto. My mother didn't want me to take the risk of being caught and punished. But after Esther died we knew we had no choice. Every day I either climbed the wall or squeezed through a hole. On the outside I bought or begged whatever food I could find. Sometimes I got bread, sometimes turnips or flour. This is what kept the rest of my family—my parents and my two other sisters—from dying of starvation like little Esther."

"The ghetto sounds terrible," I said.

"It was," Grandpa Herman answered, getting up from the table.

There were tears on his cheeks when he kissed me good night.

*t*he next morning, my grandparents and I went out into the front yard to work. But we didn't get much done. As we were kneeling down, ready to pull weeds from the flower beds, we noticed a black car driving past the house very slowly. A man and a woman were in the black car, and they were staring out the window at us.

"What could they want?" my grandmother asked. She sounded

upset. "Have we done something wrong?"

"Calm down, Trudie." Grandpa Herman patted her back to soothe her, but his face looked worried, too. "There is no reason to be afraid. A woman is in the car—no uniformed police. Maybe they are just looking at our flowers."

"You and your flowers!" My grandmother leaned back on Grandpa Herman's shoulder. "You think the whole world loves your garden as much as you do."

The sound of a car door closing made us all turn around quickly. The black car was parked in front of the house. A man dressed in a suit and tie was walking toward us.

"My wife and I were driving by on our way home," he said, "and we couldn't help admiring your beautiful garden. We just wanted to tell you how much we enjoyed it."

Grandpa Herman winked at my grandmother with an I-told-you-so look and stood up to thank the man. Soon the man's wife was out of the car and my grandfather was leading Mr. and Mrs. Lee on a tour of his garden.

"This is a flowering almond," Grandpa Herman said, touching a tree with loads of pink flowers. "It is one of the first to bloom in spring. And this is a Japanese scarlet quince…"

I walked behind my grandfather, listening as he explained how he planted some bushes and plants which bloom early and others that bloom late so there would be flowers in the yard for as many months as possible.

"You know so much, Mr. Zelkowicz!" Mrs. Lee said, clapping her hands together. Mr. Lee nodded in agreement.

"And this is what is called a butterfly bush." My grandfather pointed, showing the line of numbers above his wrist. I had seen those numbers on the same arm in the same place since I was a baby. Like the foreign accent both my grandparents spoke with, the numbers had always been a part of the Grandpa Herman and Grandma

Trudie I loved. But Mrs. Lee's face looked so surprised when she saw the numbers. It made me uneasy. I still wondered what had happened to my grandparents during the war. Were the concentration camps like prisons for criminals? Why had Grandpa Herman and Grandma Trudie been so afraid when the black car passed the house? Did they know what it felt like to be arrested?

Mr. and Mrs. Lee did not stay much longer. But before they left, my grandfather cut a branch off a bush they especially liked and gave it to Mrs. Lee.

"Plant this in your own yard," he said. "In a few years it should bloom beautifully."

Mrs. Lee was so happy with Grandpa Herman's gift, she kissed him on the cheek.

"You are a very special man, Mr. Zelkowicz," she said. "After all you have suffered, you still have room in your heart to give to strangers."

What Mrs. Lee said made me realize that she knew about the war where my grandparents got the numbers. She knew. But I didn't.

"Did you speak German when you were a little girl?" I asked Grandma Trudie that afternoon. We were standing together at the kitchen sink, peeling potatoes for supper.

"Yes," she said, "German is my mother tongue."

"What about Grandpa Herman?" I asked. "What did he speak?"

"He spoke Polish."

"Was it hard to learn another language?"

"Yes, it was hard. But we did it," Grandma Trudie answered. "Just like we made a new life for ourselves in a new country away from Europe."

few minutes later my grandmother was on her knees with her back toward me, looking in the bottom cabinet for a pan to fry the potatoes. I was glad she wasn't looking at me. It made it easier to ask my question.

"Were you ever in prison? You or Grandpa Herman?"

"Prison?" Grandma Trudie found her heavy iron skillet and stood up. "What makes you ask that, Frannie?"

"I found a striped uniform in the cedar closet. It was in a round box."

Grandma Trudie's fry pan dropped to the floor with a loud ringing crash.

For a minute I thought my grandmother was going to cry. Her face looked as sad as when she lit *yahrzeit* candles for her relatives. She took my hand in hers and stroked it.

"Let's sit down at the table, Frannie," she said.

"The thing you found is no ordinary prison uniform. It came from a Nazi concentration camp. During World War II, Nazi law made it a crime for Jewish people to live and work among the rest of the

population. First they forced all the Jews into ghettos. Then they made us prisoners in concentration camps."

Grandma Trudie paused for a moment and continued. "We were locked up behind an electrified fence and guarded with fierce dogs and soldiers with guns. They took our clothes, shaved our heads, and put numbers on our arms. We were treated like animals, not human beings. I was forced to be part of a team of women who pulled wagons like horses or donkeys."

My grandmother was guarded by dogs and soldiers with guns? I didn't like hearing these frightening things. I covered my eyes, trying to get the horrible picture out of my head—my Grandma Trudie in a striped prison uniform, with her head completely shaved, pulling a wagon.

"I don't want to hear any more," I said. Grandma Trudie was quiet. She didn't talk about the *Shoah*, the murder of six million Jews during World War II, until the next time I asked.

n another visit
Grandpa Herman told
me about hiding in the ghetto trying
to outwit the Nazis.

"In the ghetto we heard rumors
about death camps. Especially a
place called Auschwitz, which had
buildings designed for killing
thousands of people at one time. At
first the Jews did not want to
believe. They said even the Nazis
would not do anything so evil and
barbaric. But as time went on we

found out that the rumors were true. Thousands and thousands of Jews were being killed with poison gas and their bodies burned in ovens."

"My father," Grandpa Herman continued, "decided that we would not leave the ghetto and go to a death camp voluntarily. We would not report to the train station as the Nazis had ordered. My family went into hiding instead. We made a closetlike room for ourselves in an attic, and we stocked it with supplies, prepared to spend the rest of the war in this cramped little space. But the Nazis searched the houses. Our hiding place was discovered. We were captured and put with others who had also been rounded up against their will.

"A few days later we were taken to the train station and put in box cars, the kind meant for cattle. There were no seats, no toilets. There was no food. As many people as possible were crammed into each cattle car. We had to stand up. We could hardly breathe. Two days we were on this train until we finally arrived at the horrible place we had heard rumors about— *Auschwitz*.

"It was dark outside when the doors of the cattle car were opened. Guard dogs were barking. Women and children crying. Much confusion. Families were separated

by force. I was put in with a group of young men who were considered able to work. I never saw the rest of my family again. My mother and father and my two younger sisters, Anna and Elsie, were sent to the gas chambers."

"Children were killed, too?" I asked. "Just for being Jewish?"

Grandpa Herman nodded his head sadly. "One and a half million Jewish children were killed."

 year passed before I asked the next question, the one that had bothered me from the first time I heard about Jews being killed.

"Why didn't the Jews fight back? Why didn't they do something to keep the Nazis from killing them?"

"Some Jews did," Grandma Trudie said. "They organized themselves with guns and explosives, fighting with every ounce of their strength. In the

Warsaw ghetto a small number of courageous Jews fought off German troops for over a month. In Auschwitz inmates blew up one of the ovens where bodies were burned. There are many stories of Jews who fought bravely against an enemy that had at least four times as many guns and four times the ammunition."

"What about you?" I asked Grandma Trudie and Grandpa Herman. "Did you fight the Nazis?"

"Yes," Grandpa Herman said firmly. "We fought. But not with guns."

"We fought the Nazis by staying alive," Grandma Trudie said. "I cannot truly describe—and you will never be able to imagine—how difficult it was in the concentration camp. We stayed alive in a prison designed to kill its prisoners. Those who were not sent right away to the gas chambers were used as slave laborers. From early in the morning until late at night we ran heavy machinery, dug ditches, built roads, sewed uniforms—whatever work the Nazis chose for us to do. We were beaten for stopping to rest. It is quite possible to work a person to death. I saw this happen over and over again."

ittle by little I heard my grandparents' story. Each and every day in a concentration camp was an enormous struggle. It took great determination to keep living. The work was terrible, and the living conditions worse. They slept in barracks on hard wooden shelves. Insects and diseases were everywhere. They were hardly given any food—watery soup and stale bread. They were as thin as skeletons.

"To make things worse," my grandfather said, "the Nazis made us stand for hours at roll call. In the freezing rain, without coats or gloves, we would have to stand while the guards counted and recounted hundreds of prisoners. The hope that one day the Nazis would be over-thrown and I could tell my story to the world—this kept me going, kept me standing up when my body wanted so much to drop from exhaustion."

"A Jew believes in the future," Grandma Trudie added. "No matter how bad it was, we kept faith that one day the war would be over and we would have the opportunity to lead a normal life—get married, have children and grandchildren."

It hurts when I think of the way my grandparents suffered during World War II. And I get frightened when I think about so many Jewish people killed—six million. It makes me so sad to think that each person killed had a story just like Grandpa Herman and Grandma Trudie.

nce I tried to count to a million without stopping. "1,2,3,4,5,6,7,8,9,10,11,12, 13,14,15…" I got to 600 before getting mixed up. Then I tried again. "1,2,3,4,5,6,7,8,9,10,11,12,13,14,15, 16,17,18,19,20,21…" That time I counted to one thousand, looking at my wristwatch the whole time. It took me eight minutes. To count to six million would take hours and hours. That's six thousand times one thousand.

More people than I could count or even imagine were killed because they were Jewish. Why?

"There is no simple answer to that," Grandpa Herman said. "The Nazis were evil. Full of hatred. I can't understand the kind of hatred that would make someone kill an innocent child. I only know it is evil."

"Do you know the Ten Commandments?" Grandma Trudie asked me. I nodded my head. Of course I knew the commandments God gave the Israelites at Sinai. I knew them by heart and in order.

"What is commandment number six?"

"Thou shalt not kill," I answered proudly.

"Very good," Grandma Trudie said. "Then you will understand when I say that six million Jews were killed because the Nazis believed in their leader, Adolf Hitler, before anything else. When a human being is given the power to decide what is good and what is evil, the world is in chaos—crazy. Hitler said that certain people were not worthy of life, and his followers obeyed his orders without question. The Nazis showed us what kind of world we have when the Ten Commandments, God's laws, are disregarded."

 still visit my grandparents whenever I can. We still walk to synagogue on Shabbat and work in the garden on Sundays. Every once in a while I go down to the cedar closet to look at the grey striped shirt. Grandpa Herman says it will belong to me someday. He wants me to show it to MY grandchildren. "You must tell them our story," he said. I promised I would.

Author's Note:

Resistance is another word for fighting. In this story, Grandma Trudie and her family resisted the Nazis by moving to Holland after Hitler took power in Germany. Grandpa Herman and his family resisted by smuggling food into the ghetto and by hiding when the Nazis ordered them to report to the train station.

They both resisted by not giving up hope during their terrible days in the concentration camps. Every European Jew who struggled to survive—whether successful or not—fought a courageous battle against incredible odds.